'With masterful lyricism and elegant language, Emilienne Malfatto gives an account of one of the intimate tragedies that so often pass unnoticed between falling bombs.' – *Libération*

'Approaching the tragedy of femicide from the inside, Emilienne Malfatto brings a stripped back lyricism to these destinies of submission.' – *Livres Hebdo*

'The writing is simple, the sentences often short and arresting. The story comes swift and powerful, a true literary achievement.' – *France Info*

'A long poem in prose, like a fable, or Greek tragedy. A beautiful book, and beautiful first novel.' – *France bleue*

'A hard-hitting tale of many voices, that is strong, moving and painful in equal measure.' – *Femmes ici et ailleurs*

'A first novel that reads raw, laid bare, short and hard-hitting. A taut tragedy, like a rope that we know is fragile, threatened by obscurantism, the weight of tradition and taboo. A deep dive into present day Iraq.' – Bernard Magnier, *Le français dans le monde*

Emilienne Malfatto

MAY THE TIGRIS GRIEVE FOR YOU

*Translated from the French
by Lorna Scott Fox*

Les Fugitives
London

This first English-language edition published by Les Fugitives editions in the United Kingdom in April 2023 · Les Fugitives Ltd, 91 Cholmley Gardens, Fortune Green Road, West Hampstead, London NW6 1UN · www.lesfugitives.com · Originally published as *Que sur toi se lamente le Tigre* © Éditions Elyzad, 2020 · Published by arrangement with Agence littéraire Astier-Pécher ALL RIGHTS RESERVED · English-language translation © Lorna Scott Fox, 2023 · Cover design and illustration by Sarah Schulte · Text design by MacGuru Ltd · All rights reserved · No part of this publication may be reproduced, stored in a retrieval system or transmitted in any form or by any means, electronic, mechanical, photocopying, recording or otherwise, without prior permission in writing from Les Fugitives editions · A CIP catalogue record for this book is available from the British Library · The rights of Emilienne Malfatto to be identified as author, and the rights of Lorna Scott Fox to be identified as translator of this work have been identified in accordance with Section 77 of the Copyright, Designs and Patents Act 1988 · Printed in England by CMP, Poole, Dorset · ISBN · 978-1-8384904-9-2 · This book has received financial support from the Institut français as part of its foreign rights acquisition Programme d'Aide à la Publication.

MAY THE TIGRIS GRIEVE FOR YOU

For the women of the Euphrates:
Maryam, Shadia, Alia.

To Tiktum and Fatma, who do not yet know
that their freedom will end.

Siduri says to Gilgamesh:
'Gilgamesh, where are you hurrying to?
You will never find that life you seek.
When the gods created man, they destined him for death.

It came like a wave. A groundswell rising from the depths of me. I didn't understand at first. The earth was shaking inside my belly. Like a blow against a door, like a tidal wave. I didn't want to understand. I looked up. Doves were wheeling in circles under the clouds. The wave inside receded. The sky teetered. I fell onto my hands in the dust, among the black veils. A cotton hem stroked my cheek. The second kick came, the second thunderclap, the second earthquake. At that moment, on the ground, among the black veils, in the dust, I understood. And the universe came crashing down.

Death is inside me. It came along with life. These blows to my belly, this rending of the flesh are bearers of death and death is on its way. It will arrive in a little while, at sunset, I will hear its rather heavy step, somewhat lopsided, limping slightly, and then the door at the end of the corridor will open and death will enter.

We are born in blood, we become a woman in blood, we give birth in blood. And in a little while there will be blood, too. As though the earth had not drunk enough of women's blood. As though the land of Iraq still thirsted for death, for blood, for innocence. Babylon has not had its fill of blood. I stood for a long time by the river, waiting to see the waters run red.

I am the Tigris. For thousands of moons I have coursed through the desert, long as a sacred vein. I flow from up there, from the mountains, I drop down to the plain, then the desert, then into the far-off sea, like a breath.

I am life and I am death. I am the beginning and the end. I am the crops and the floods. I am the tears of Tiamat slain by the hand of Marduk.

I know men's folly. I have seen them a thousand times brought low by vanity. I saw the rise of Ashur and Nineveh and the fall of great kings, and the rain of Gilgamesh drowned my banks. All of them returned to dust. Marduk created the world from a corpse.

I bear silent witness to the pledges and dramas played out on my shores. This story, too, will end badly. Death will come in time.

I pushed myself up, both hands flat in the dust. A veil fallen from the line made a great black blotch on the ground. I thought of a pool of dried blood. I wiped my grey hands and gathered the fallen cloth. At my feet there was laundry to hang, but I could no longer see. The sun and the stars had gone dark. All that remained was this lurching in my gut, these kicks, this deadly life.

My one memory of our one embrace is a memory of fear and pain. Fear of someone knocking or of my brothers waking up; it would have meant death for us both. And the pain in my belly, in my sex, all over, the tearing of my flesh, already. There was no pleasure, it was a hurried, dismal embrace. Mohammed possessed me the way a drunken soldier goes into battle, blindly, clumsily, unstoppably.

I didn't say no, I didn't say yes. It was our day for meeting, when Mother goes to Najaf to visit my father's grave, Layla is at school and

my brothers are asleep. Every time, two quick
raps on the outer gate: it was him. We would
shut ourselves into the green bedroom, the
one nearest the door, where Layla and I sleep.
Every time we went a little further. Every
time we felt a little scared of straying into the
forbidden, of getting caught. I liked feeling
his hands on my back, his lips on my hair, my
closeness to him. I thought I was safe.

That Friday he arrived later than usual,
slightly out of breath. He had to go back to
Mosul before noon, he'd only just found out.
He became insistent, cajoling, demanding.
He went over to check the door was bolted.
He said it didn't count, he was going back to
war, and anyway we'd get engaged during his
next leave. We could allow ourselves a small
advance on that, he said, it was a matter of
living and not waiting.

Straight afterwards I felt afraid. The sense
of an irreversible mistake, a curse. A
premonition. I didn't tell him. I told him
to go. At the door, I clung to his neck with
both arms, as if drowning. Like a child. I was
scared. Our two deaths were written, there,
on the side of that black gate. He loosened my

knotted arms, kissed my hands and left. On returning to the room, I could feel my blood and his sperm on my thighs. Blood and milk, life and death. There was a stain on the rug, I had to lie to Baneen, I told her my period had come.

And then my periods stopped coming. The first month I hardly noticed, it sometimes happened. The following months I thought it was because of grief. I thought Mohammed's death had dried me up. When Father died I didn't bleed either, not for months. It's because of sadness, the doctor said when Mother finally took me to see him. He looked at me kindly, intently, while she was talking about the worry of having an 'abnormal' daughter. It was already shame enough to be seeing the doctor about *that*, may the neighbours never find out, how could they find out, but that was one of my mother's great dreads. The doctor reassured her, called her *Ma'am* and said the bleeding would return when my grief had subsided. He had seen several such cases since the war began. 'Psychosomatic,' he said, but we didn't know that word in Arabic.

My name is Tigris but I spring each day from Taurus and the tempest, high in the mountains of the North. The men of those regions have slashed my flank, abraded my course with metal and pickaxes. They built walls of steel and cement to constrict my waters. They are like the wind in the rushes, they pass through but will not endure. When you count in millennia, as I do, nothing matters very much at all.

I hung out the rest of the washing. I could see over our alley to the city rooftops. Everywhere the same black veils pegged out to dry. Everywhere the biting sunlight. By leaning out I could just glimpse the Tigris, long, sluggish, silent, with its smell of wetness and rotting grass. When first we came here from Baghdad, it was my favourite place. I used to sit on the banks and watch the fishermen pull up glistening netfuls of carp. In summer, young boys would bathe there, gesticulating among sprays of silver. I did not bathe, I remained on the edge. I've forever had this sense of being on the edge of life. Then came the blood, that first, sticky stain almost black between my legs, and Mother said that from now on I must *learn proper manners*, stop gadding about and cover my pigtails. And then one evening Amir tossed me a big black cloak and said that from now on I must wear the abaya. Nobody turned a hair. My brother Ali frowned and I thought he was about to say something, to ward off the black cloak. But he kept quiet, gazed at me briefly with a mixture of pity and shame, and lowered his eyes, to avoid mine. After that I was no longer allowed to sit on the banks of the Tigris.

I hung the rest of the washing and climbed down the wooden ladder. Already the wind was scorching hot.

I told Baneen I needed to go to the hospital. She cupped a hand to her rounded belly. Amir's child. Life. She was annoyed: to go out in her condition, in this heat, the very idea, unthinkable. For me to go alone was doubly unthinkable, forbidden, worse, an offence to both honour and modesty. I insisted. I couldn't wait for my brothers to come home, or my mother. I had to know, to be sure, that the blade was truly falling. I made things up at random, dizziness, pains, haemorrhages. Baneen sighed. She eyed me suspiciously, she's not a fool. With the slight waddle pregnancy has given her, she went to fetch her abaya.

The hospital is by the river. It smells of chlorine, sweat and medicine. Everything in it is dirty. A nurse asked Baneen to wait outside, where the vendors tack between the benches. I lay down on a blue cot. The sheet was soiled with dark blotches that made me think of blood. An old woman lay supine in a corner, wordless, soundless, as if she was dying without bothering a soul.

The nurse was elderly. Grey strands escaped the looseness of her veil. She hardly spoke as she guided the stethoscope. After a long, sorrowful look at me, she called for a doctor. The only woman doctor here is away, she explained, so you'll have to be examined by a man. I thought of Baneen, outside, who would never have agreed.

The doctor was from Baghdad, you could tell by his accent. Very young, copper-polished under his pale blue gown. He gently palpated my stomach. His hands felt light. They were met by kicks. He didn't need to ask me anything. He straightened up, removed his glasses and wiped them at length on the corner of his gown. He suddenly seemed much older, and infinitely tired. He put his glasses on and looked at me. Five months, perhaps more. The nurse didn't move. My unmarried status was on my file. And so it was like a death sentence. With those four words, the doctor had placed my head on the block.

I heard my sentence as if through a wad of cotton. My body was now nothing but a womb.

The doctor began speaking again, leaning towards me. I think he tried to understand. His eyes were disconsolate. He used strange words, *denial*, and again, *psychosomatic*. The nurse had taken my hand. I thought of my mother, who would alert Amir herself if she got the chance. Honour matters more than life. With us, sooner a dead daughter than a single mother. The doctor asked me what I was going to do, whether I had any family somewhere else, far from here. I wanted to tell him they were all dead, and those who weren't dead would kill me. The words remained blocked in my belly.

Baneen

I am the wife, the submissive woman, the decent woman, who respects the rules and will not question them. Who cannot conceive of their being disrespected. I am she who watches, judges, and condemns. She who applauds society and glorifies her husband. I will not hold back the arm of vengeance. Later, in the night, I will not see him as a murderer but as a strong man.

I am Amir's wife. We sleep in the big pink bedroom. The first night – our wedding night – the room smelled of fresh paint. I had received gifts of satin sheets and gold.

This marriage was not forced on me. On the contrary, much weeping was needed to secure it. My brothers were against it. He is too violent a man, too conservative, they said of Amir when he came seeking my hand. As for me, I dreamed of his black eyes and broad shoulders. Here, women conceal their bodies, but young men bathe half naked. And young women watch them silently, out of the corner of their veils.

My father gave in and so did my brothers. I married Amir. I came to live in his house, in the pink bedroom. He had painted the walls himself.

He married me in wartime, between two battles. His hands were calloused and abrupt. He touched me as one touches a weapon. The first night he was unable to penetrate me. He shook. He lost his temper, punched the wall. I kept quiet. At last he fell asleep on the bed, a heavy, deep sleep that had something animal about it. His breathing was like the snorting of buffaloes. I didn't dare to go to sleep. I felt fearful of this too-strong man stretched out beside me. Tonight, in the hollow of darkness, in the blackness of the bedroom, will I fear him again?

On the second night he succeeded. He hurt me. I had been forewarned. Women are expected to hurt, it proves that their husband is all man. After that he held me, briefly and tenderly, in his powerful arms. In the morning he had to go back to the front. The sheet was blotched with blood. A brownish flower, almost black. Honour had been preserved.

I am gentle and meek, I wear the veil at home in front of my brothers-in-law, I am a seemly wife. I don't laugh too loud or speak out of turn. A respectable woman.

I am she who asks no questions and upsets nobody. Who accepts her condition, never imagining the possibility of a different life. I sweep the floor with plaited reeds. I sweeten my husband's tea. I make my face up every evening before he comes home.

I am the woman who carries an unborn child, the child who will be born. I am the woman who will live, because she has accepted to live within society's limits. I am perhaps the happiest of all.

Khorsabad, Nineveh. Mosul. I wind through fields of ruins. In the great city of the North, I flow past shattered houses. A giant has trampled the streets. Even the stones suffered here. The concrete screamed, the metal wailed. The city of men became a blasted anthill, heaps of rubble poised to slide into my stream. The men in black left nothing but ashes behind. But they too returned to dust. My waters ran red awhile beneath the broken bridges.

The gods, when they created Man, embedded death in him. Before Gilgamesh's eyes, the serpent seized eternal life. Enkidu remained as dust.

The first time the world turned red, I was nine years old. My father had given in to my passionate pleas to take me with him to the writers' quarter. We hadn't left the house for eight months, shut in till he got home at night, while Layla cried and my brothers squabbled. The least delay and my mother would go berserk, wringing her hands, raging at the portrait of Imam Ali. Bearded and sovereign next to his lion, he seemed to disdain her.

Father didn't want to take me, he had already been caught in the vicinity of an attack. Twice. But that day he agreed.

Once outside, I didn't recognise Baghdad. The city had been partitioned by concrete walls, everyone walked fast, tanks were stationed on every corner like big insects lying in wait. Weapons everywhere. People's faces hardened by distrust and fear. The palm trees beheaded. Even the light seemed different, greyish-yellow and grubby.

Turning into Mutanabbi Street, Father held my hand tight. It was the crowded hour. In spite of the war, the attacks, the Americans, some booksellers had set out their displays. Just before we started down the street, Father stopped me for a lecture. 'You stick close to me, Baghdad is not what it was, it's dangerous these days. I'll just find my book and we'll go home.' I nodded, yes Daddy, whatever you say. I believe he was scared. I was, too, this whole world was beginning to spook me. What was the point of going out if I had to scurry along with my hand in a vice, unable to wander off or play or pester for a book, an ice lolly, a bracelet. At the corner, we had to stop for a cart piled high with oranges. A dull green car was parked by the kerb; I drew a star in the dust of the windshield with my finger.

Three displays on, Father found his book. He showed it to me, grinning. I can't remember the title, but the cover was blue. He grasped my hand again, tightly, and the universe exploded. The world went black then red. I fell backwards. I saw Father fall too. I was deaf, head spinning, lungs full of fiery dust, eyes burning. My clothes all grey with ash. Father throwing up beside me. A pillar of black smoke rose into the sky and the torn, singed pages of books spiralled on the wind.

Everything happened very fast and everything seemed stilled, crystallised in a metallic murk. I thought the sun would never come out again. All around us people were running. At the corner, where the dull green car had exploded, a bonfire leaped. Directly opposite, by the side of the road, a little girl was screaming, clutching her mother's hand. There was no arm attached. The mother was just a lump of flesh and metal, a swarming magma, red and black. And the child was covered in that blood in that blood in that blood like an open wound and screaming for her mother to wake up and the hand was dangling from the end of her own arm.

When we were small, my brothers used to catch lizards in the courtyard of our house and we'd cut off their tails in the hope of seeing them grow back, which never happened. Now the children of my country ask their mother if their arm will grow back. We are the land of the maimed and the bleeding, the land of shadows and phantoms. Abdallah, who had a tea stall on our street, he's dead. Sarah, who

went to buy oranges the day of an attack,
she's dead. Dead, the mother once attached
to the hand. Dead, dead, dead, and I will be
dead soon. By the hand of those closest to me.
Escape, where to, what for? My body weighs
too heavily, my veins are filled with lead.

Enkidu does not lift his eyes again.
When Gilgamesh touches his heart, it does not beat.
Then Gilgamesh lays a veil, as one veils a bride, over his friend.
He begins to rage like a lion, like a lioness robbed of her cubs.
This way and that he paces around the bed, tears his hair and strews it on the ground.
He pulls off his splendid robes and flings them away from him as though they were abominations.

The big coffin that brought Mohammed home was empty. The men in green headbands unloaded it from the car without effort. The box was draped in a smooth, shiny, emerald-green flag. The fighters' faces were inscrutable; Mohammed's mother tore at her breast. Hassan, my youngest and sweetest brother, described the scene to me. Amir would never have let me attend.

That night, the Kalashnikovs popped until late. With every martyr, men shoot at the stars and women rip their veils.

Amir came home with the coffin. He'd known Mohammed since they were small, we had all left Baghdad together. It was he who told me the news. Ali also knew. The telephone had rung during the night, and Ali avoided my gaze the next day. Amir walked in smelling of death, his eyes hollow and a bit crazed. By then, I hadn't bled for a month. I knew what he was going to say before he said it. The ground gave under me. The earth shook, I swear. The walls pitched sideways. I clung to the wall and Amir reached out his hands to catch me, he who so rarely showed affection. He knew we loved each other; he had given his blessing to our forthcoming engagement.

The empty shroud was buried in dry earth, this earth of ours that never seems sated with blood. Mohammed's body remained in Mosul, cinders upon cinders, burned, pulverised, wiped out by the bomb that flattened the building on Farooq Street.

Amir

I am the brother and the dealer of death.
I am the man of the family, the eldest, the
repository of male authority – the only
authority that matters, that has ever mattered.
I am the brother who shouldered the father's
mantle. I reign over the women.

I am the killer. Soon I will kill, but I don't
know that yet. What would I do if I knew?
Would I turn on my heel in the dusty
alleyway? Soon I will kill, believing that
I had no choice. Her life or our honour.
It is not I who will kill, but the street, the
neighbourhood, the town. This whole country.

Soon I will kill, for the first time. The men I
killed in war don't count, they're nameless
and faceless. Their deaths are our lives. Our
victories. I learned this during the war and
more besides. The hands that quake after
battle, the bottomless icy terror that paralyses
or maddens, or whips some to an orgasm of

fire – those who think themselves invincible and die the next second. I learned cold and heat, filth and pestilence. Rats and dogs and cats unhinged by the din of war and human meat. The belly like an iron claw. Piss running down the leg, that no one talks about. The whistle of the shell and the wadded deafness after it explodes. The laughter, too raucous to be real, the solidarity of men-at-arms, and the thought that comes on hearing a plane – *let it bomb anywhere but here.* We call ourselves brothers, but we have never been more alone. Let them all perish, so long as I survive.

Mohammed was like my brother, and yet on seeing his body I felt unnerved and strangely relieved. *It could have been me.* You don't say such things aloud, but you think them, down there on the ground in the mud. War isn't noble or grand or brave, war is frightened men sprawled flat in sludge and muck, praying to God they will not die. Being allowed to live in peace, that's luxury.

I came back from the war, but every night the planes are with me. They circle above, invade the pink bedroom, vibrate inside my head. I came back, but the planes visit every night. I

stare up at the ceiling, waiting for the bomb
that never drops, I flee from the room, from
my wife's gentle gaze and soft arms, too soft,
I walk the streets, I sit down by the side of the
great river. I pass other men who are like me.
We've become a land of insomniacs. At dawn,
the planes go away and I can sleep at last.

I survived the war and tonight I will kill. In
killing I will die a little. But my arm will not
tremble.

Will it?

On my bank there is a tree that comes from Eden. Eve picked the apple from that tree. The forbidden tree, the tree of knowledge.

Men believe in it. The tree is spindly and dried-up, surrounded by a fence. It has witnessed every war on earth. And yet men still tie coloured ribbons to it, and twists of paper, begging for life and peace.

Hassan had listened to the militiamen as they talked, in between praying and weeping, during the three nights of the funeral wake. Amir and his *brothers*-in-arms described what happened. Hassan didn't want to tell me at first, but then he gave in. Mohammed's death came on wings of steel with the scream of metal.

It was morning. The mist was lifting over the Tigris. They moved forwards in small groups, crouching, scurrying, inflamed, euphoric, fearful. Sometimes they came across civilians with eyes like ghosts. The children sobbed loudly or made no sound, the women hid, the men emerged with their hands in the air. The pop of weapons, then the very particular stillness of war, that thick, muffled silence, cold as fog. In the big city of the North, people had been afraid for a long time. Brother had betrayed brother, neighbour had denounced neighbour. Four sons in one family had joined different camps and killed each other.

The city reeked of death. It was a bland, sweetish odour, slightly queasy and metallic. The stink of carrion. Inside your nostrils, under your clothes, under your nails, under your skin. The smell-memory of death. That smell never washes off. It strikes without warning as you're eating or sleeping, when making love it wafts in to fill your nose, your head, your room, and there you are, back on Farooq Street in Mosul, among the corpses left to rot.

The rumble of metal was already up there in the sky. But the noise was reassuring. The former adversaries were now helping us to fight the new enemy. No one ever saw them. They struck from way up high, wounding the blue with bombs and steel. Like droning insects, distant, out of reach. A few days earlier the men in black had downed an army helicopter. The blazing bird fell onto the city. After that, joyful volleys crackled into the small hours in *their* parts of town. In wartime, men celebrate death as they do life in times of peace.

They were edging along Farooq Street. Bullets thudded. Two sharp reports, a sniper.

Mohammed's group sought shelter in a building. The facade was gaping, the upper storeys spewing twisted chunks of concrete and tangled metal rods. One column seemed to hang in empty space, ceilings holding on by a thread. In war the laws of matter change.

Up there the metal was still droning. It happened very fast. The sky ripped, a whistle, a white bolt of lightning, or maybe red or black, the men couldn't tell, the colours got mixed up in their accounts. The concrete was falling. A fraction of a second's suspense. The end of the world. A mistaken target.

There was no body to collect, to wash, to weep over. They laid some clothes in the coffin, the black keffiyeh he sometimes wore. I think they lied about it to his mother.

Mohammed

I am dead. I lie under concrete and metal. My body is contorted, my neck broken. Someone very far away, high up in the sky, or sitting at a disembodied screen even farther away, someone mistook a building, a street, a neighbourhood, a uniform. I died by mistake. What a stupid way to go. I dreamed of being a hero, I wound up as collateral damage.

I am dead and I will never be a father, never be a husband, nevermore a lover or a friend. My body has already decomposed, and yet I remember the strength of my arms and the desire that sometimes gleamed in girls' eyes when we, the boys, bathed in the great river among sprays of silver. I am carrion, but I can't forget the green bedroom.

I am dead and my death will lead to other deaths. The woman whom I wanted for my pleasure. My child, who will not be born. My gratification meant their punishment. In this land of sand and scorpions, women pay the price on men's behalf.

I watched the men in black. They came from the west, up in arms, vociferating. At first, they found a way to manage men and crowds. June saw the last cigarettes smoked on my banks. In July, darkness fell on Nineveh.

Amir will return home tonight, and death will enter this house with him. Death will have a tired face and a slightly dragging, lopsided step. My brother has walked with a limp ever since he took a bullet in the leg on the bridge at Tikrit.

Amir still does not know that he's a murderer.

Death is on its way. It left Mosul in one of those big white cars with tinted windows, packed with weapons and fighters, the stern faces of imams painted on the great flags rippling in their wake.

He called Baneen just now, they'd passed Baghdad.

Baneen knows. She holds it against me that she knows. She never asked, she didn't say anything. She feels torn between her wifely duty and her pity for me. Her womb bears life as mine bears death. It is her first child. Amir is overjoyed at becoming a father.

They have been married a year, she hasn't encountered his violence yet. She only knows his powerful muscles, his black beard, and the pink bedroom they share at the back of the house.

It was a war wedding. Amir returned to the front two days later, greeted by knowing winks and brawny backslaps, spoiling for the fight, replete, relieved to be a man at last.

Amir chose well, my mother says. Baneen is *a fine wife*. She doesn't leave the house or speak too loud; she knows her place. She anticipates her husband's every desire. Baneen is a bustling shadow in a veil. She keeps busy in the kitchen, in the bedrooms, with the household tasks that are her universe and in which she becomes absorbed and loses herself until dissolving altogether.

Hassan

I am he who is not yet a man. The kid brother, the boy who still belongs to the world of women. They don't wear their veils in front of me. That will come later. I am my sister's favourite and the one who will miss her the most.

If I could, if I were a man, I would stop the killer's arm.

I am the sweet, affectionate one; I haven't yet internalised all the rules of manhood. Will I escape that straitjacket? Will I grow up to be a killer, like my brother? Or will I break out of this awful, dark, constricted world? All the young men around here want to leave. There's no future here, they say, sitting by the river. Look at our wives, our sisters, our daughters, the boldest ones say, it's terrible to see them got up like black ghosts. But they, too, jealously guard the honour of their sisters, wives and daughters. They too would kill if they had to, like my brother must tonight.

Here everybody wants to leave, but not many
do. Violence deters us from the big cities,
while borders are closed to our passport the
colour of mourning. And so we stay here by
the river, glad at least to be nowhere near the
men in black and their madness.

I am the boy whose future is still unwritten.
I am the one who might not become a
murderer.

My waters were poisoned a long time ago. My stream is wide and full, my banks are rich in loam, but little by little I am dying. Because men have long since ceased to love me or respect me. They have acquired a taste for disaster.

I am no longer a source but a resource, and the men of this parched land have forgotten that they cannot live without me. They will perish with me, because our fates are intertwined.

Amir was six years old when I was born.
When our father died, he was sixteen.
He took over Father's place and his authority.
But never, neither in his eyes nor in his voice,
nor in his demeanour, did he show any of the
gentleness my father had and which I seemed
to recognise, at times, in Mohammed.

When I was little, I didn't much like
Mohammed. I didn't like any of Amir's friends.
They shooed me away from their games with a
kind of derision; the inquisitive glances came
later. Mohammed was one of them. He was
thin and dark, quiet, somewhat withdrawn. He
bred doves up on the roof. I can see them now,
wheeling in white circles above his head. He
lived next door on Fellah Street, in Madinat
as-Saddam. Our grimy suburb, grey with dust,
draped in flags of black and red and green.
Mourning, jihad, faith. The trinity of the
destitute. Regime change brought a change
of name. Saddam was replaced by Muqtada,
but the destitution remained. Nowadays they
call it Madinat as-Sadr, *Sadr City*, and the
Americans fear it.

Mohammed was an only child. His mother Latifa often treated me to cardamom and date pastries. On feast days, her laughter rang out all around the block. His father had lost an arm on the Iranian front, before any of us were born. He used to sit for hours staring at the wall, sunk in thought. Latifa was cheerful enough for both of them.

When we left Baghdad, they left with us. It rained that day. The sky was dirty and blurred, icy tears washing away my mother's as she closed the door behind us. Father had died a week earlier. His heart stopped in the night. The previous day he had found himself yet again in the radius of an attack. He came home white as parchment, out of breath, his hands clenched against his chest. He died that night.

He was buried the next day at Wadi Salaam, in Najaf. A hole in the ground among millions of others. I felt hurt for Father when the spadefuls of earth fell onto the white sheet. I wanted the earth to make itself light for him. Mother seemed out of her mind, Amir and Ali had to hold her back on the edge of the hole. Mohammed was there with his father. They didn't say anything. Hassan was crying softly. I held Layla in my arms. An old man recited prayers over the grave. Afterwards he had to be paid. It was Mohammed who pulled out some banknotes.

That evening, back in Baghdad, Latifa was waiting for us, huge and maternal. She wrapped Mother in her arms and cradled her like a baby. Then they shut themselves away together, while Mohammed talked to Amir, Ali and his father. They were deciding to leave Baghdad.

Madinat as-Salaam. The city of peace has become the city of war, of concrete, of blood. How great was its splendour once. My banks were studded with palm trees and palaces. I bathed caliphs and long-tressed princesses. Now, Baghdad in agony disgorges all of its bile and its wounded into me.

We travelled south. Mohammed's old car bumped along the river road between the palm groves. Amir had managed to borrow another car to carry what remained of us and our belongings. Mother took my father's suits but not the big portrait of Imam Ali, who had failed to protect us. Layla and I were in Mohammed's car with his parents. His father sat in front, in the passenger seat. I could see his truncated shoulder, his missing arm. Mohammed drove in silence, his jaw set hard. When we got into the car, in Baghdad, he'd looked back at the house, and I think there were tears in his eyes. Before leaving, he had opened the doves' cage on the roof. The birds hadn't wanted to come out. He was seventeen.

All around stretched ashen desert. The roadside was littered with burnt-out cars. The world looked yellowy-grey in that eerie end-of-winter light that feels like the end of all things. In the palm groves the towering silhouettes of trees decapitated by war reached as far as the eye could see. Like vanquished, emaciated soldiers, like an army of dead men in the sands.

Every hour or so, an American or army checkpoint made us slow down and stop. The men got out with their hands on their heads, the women stayed together. I was ten, I didn't wear a veil yet.

At one checkpoint, a fair-haired soldier yelled at the men in a foreign language. The black barrel of his gun jabbed at us scornfully. He made the men kneel down, just for fun, just to humiliate. When we set off again, Mohammed spat out of the window.

It was evening when we arrived. The street was pitch-black – power cuts were as frequent here as in Baghdad. You couldn't hear any of the noises of war, just the last birds chirping and the muffled grunts of buffaloes, their snorting breaths. The air smelled different, damper. In the distance the lights of a town that was not Baghdad were reflected in the curve of the Tigris.

We were expected. A woman in a black abaya appeared, like a ghost in the night. She hugged the women, kissed Layla and Hassan and stroked my hair. Then she led us to a small house where we could stay until we found something better. She was my father's sister.

The Mother

I am the mother, the prematurely aged woman whose shapeless body hides under black cloths, whose mouth is toothless from too many children, whose hair is always covered, even behind closed doors. I am that dim, graceless form, I totter like an old crone and I'm not even fifty years old.

My life has crept by behind walls and veils, in submission to men, in this peculiar women's world that acts like a deforming mirror on people and things.

My life is behind me, and I don't know what I've lived. I slid over joys and sorrows by accepting my lot; I married the man assigned to me, bore children, endured wars. With each child, each war, each casual slight inflicted by this world made for men, I stooped lower, bowed beneath black veils. I have not laughed for longer than I can say.

I am old, and to me my children's world is alien. I conscientiously applied to my daughters the rules that had been imposed on me. Around them I built the same prison as my own. I justified my world by reproducing it.

I am not lacking in maternal love, but it grew dulled by prohibitions and obligations, beneath the veils and the frustrations. Was I loved in my adult life? Did I love the father of my children? I pushed such questions away because they were pointless, because my mother taught me not to ask them. Because around me she built the same prison as her own.

Did I ever dream of something different? A different life, other possibilities? Did I ever lie awake beside my older husband, imagining a throbbing deep inside and whispered vows to some faceless young man? If I did once dream, I no longer remember it. Our world is not made for dreams.

I am the mother, and I am not there, but in the valley of the dead, calcified in piety and the prescribed mourning over my husband's grave. My daughter is going to be killed. Will Amir wait till I get home? It's a long journey in the pilgrims' coach. My son is going to kill my daughter and I won't stop him. Would I stop him if I did return in time? I've accepted the rules for much too long by now.

To the South, my wound, my soul. Already once my weakening stream retreated from the reedbeds where the lions and gazelles of yore would come to slake their thirst.

Here the two veins of Mesopotamia converge. The great salt-lands of Sumer, plied by silver barques.

For a long time, I considered Mohammed as no more than a friend of my brother's, someone who was a bit quiet, a bit sullen. I'm desperately trying to recall the exact moment when I first noticed the velvet in his eyes. Which exact movement of his kept me awake at night, my thoughts locked on him, my belly fluttering. Since his death I have forgotten all of it. My memory is blanketed in ash. The more I try to summon up his face, the more it eludes me. The contours are blurred, I can't make out his eyes. He is terribly far away.

He spoke the first words at the hottest time of day, in summer, when men and beasts are demolished by the heat and the wind burns your eyes and lips. He didn't usually visit at that time. He'd show up earlier or later, the friendly neighbour, all smiles, knocking loudly on the gate to announce his presence and give us women time to cover our hair and safeguard our honour. Men, too, respect the rules.

That day Amir had gone out, I can't remember where Mother was. It was during the peace, before Iraq was devoured once more by war. Amir and Mohammed hadn't yet enlisted in the militia. They did odd jobs in cafés or on building sites. Work was scarce; men with nothing to do slept late, then whiled away the time playing dominos. In the evening they roamed the riverbank for hours. Women had no such leisure. The housework never ends.

I went to school in the mornings. Everything seemed normal. I already loved Mohammed. For several months I hadn't dared to look him in the face. Each hour was a dreary, interminable waiting for him to arrive. And then he was there, and the universe fell into place. I'd bring the tea tray in with lowered eyes.

That day, he ruffled Layla's hair, joked with Ali, and teased Hassan as he was getting ready for school. My brothers left the house, Mohammed stayed behind to wait for Amir. He was sitting in the green bedroom, where since morning the mattresses had been folded and stowed on top of the wardrobe. The air was sticky and close, the ceiling fan

unbearably motionless. He drank his tea in
little sips. He didn't speak to me. I felt the wall
against my back. My stomach in a vice.

Suddenly he asked if I remembered Baghdad,
Fellah Street, the ice-cream seller in summer.
He began to reminisce about our childhood.
I looked at him as he sat opposite me on the
bare floor. He was utterly beautiful, utterly
alive. Since my father's death it was as if the
whole house had died, and Mother too. The
darkness had pervaded us. Mohammed was a
gust of life.

He hadn't grown a beard yet, his cheeks were
angular and bare. He became animated, his
long hands drew Baghdad in the warm air.
Streets, grids, the big Kadhimiya intersection.
The riverside casinos, casting their lights into
the water and spreading the scent of narghile,
the easeful life of men amid the rattle of dice
and the clack of dominos. Families picnicking
on Abu Nuwas, Ottoman balconies and infinite
wheeling of doves in the sky. He conjured
all this up for me, for himself, with glowing
eyes. I fastened avidly on his black gaze, his
long eyelashes, his gestures. He wore just
one ring, on his left hand. A turquoise set in

silver. And then, just as he was going along
Rasheed Street with its cinemas and vendors,
its bomb-free sky and portraits of Saddam, he
stopped short, as if he'd only just noticed me.
He lowered his eyes. He said it in a low voice,
almost not saying it. *You've grown beautiful.*

I didn't say anything, didn't know how, didn't
dare. Outside, the black gate clanged. Amir's
step was not yet lopsided. I tightened my veil
and slipped from the green bedroom and deep
into the house so that my brother could not
guess at my elation, my treachery. My breach
of honour. Later, when I brought in the tea,
I felt Mohammed's surreptitious eyes on me
when Amir wasn't looking.

Later, much later, he gave me the turquoise
ring set in silver. It was too big, too loose
on every finger. I hung it on a chain, a long
one, to avoid questions from my mother and
brothers. Amir would have recognised the
ring.

*She bares her breasts, makes herself naked
and welcomes his eagerness;
Enkidu rejoices in her body's charms.
She makes herself naked, and as he falls upon
her she teaches this wild man, this innocent,
the woman's art.
For six days and seven nights he possesses
her, forgetting his home in the hills.
And when he is satisfied, he turns back
to the beasts, his old companions.
But when the gazelles see him, they bolt
away; when the wild creatures see him
they flee.*

Tikrit had changed him. Mohammed returned with the spring, alive, but something in him had died. For a long time I searched for the man I loved, in his eyes that had turned shifty and clouded, in his hands, grown limper yet more aggressive. The rumble of war had reached us, floating down the river on tales of battles, massacres, torched houses and raped women.

He and Amir had joined up together. The two friends became brothers-in-arms. They were each issued with a green headband and a Kalashnikov. The city's young men departed in droves, responding to the call of the turbans, securing their place in Paradise, defending our sanctuaries, our land, against the men in black.

I disliked the militiamen with their strident laughter, conquering airs and severe, judgemental eyes that seemed to bore through women's veils – the veils they had themselves prescribed and then seemed to lift off with their gaze. They think they have a monopoly on honour and virility. A monopoly on God.

Convoys rolled one after another down the road, decked in flags showing Imam Ali or Imam Hussain, beautiful, appalling, bloodied. Men acted a little crazy on their return, still carrying their weapons, prone to fighter's reactions or deathly silences. They moved through their homes like invaders or hunted beasts. Some of them cried out in their sleep at night, pursued in dreams by bombs or by the men in black or by corpses with no eyes.

Sometimes, in the green bedroom, Mohammed would tell me things. He spoke of Fallujah, Ramadi, Jalawla. Of fear, exhaustion, dirt and hunger. Death had crept under his skin. Sometimes he apologised for having brought death into our house. Once he asked whether his smell had changed. He was sure he gave off that sweetish carrion scent of blood and metal. He would lift my veil and breathe in my hair; it smelled like sand, he said.

After Tikrit, he never told me anything again. I didn't ask. Perhaps I should have. Tikrit had put a barrier between us. I didn't want to know. I was afraid. I dreaded finding out that he, too, was a murderer. That he had looted, raped, burned. That he had killed, not in the heat of battle, but coldly. The way Amir will kill me in a little while. Then Mohammed died, and now I am alone with these uncertainties and that death inside. What does it matter, after all. We kill, we are killed. We are a country of victims and murderers.

My waters once buoyed ships and winged bulls and kings. For many seasons now, they have borne men. Pallid, riddled, bloated bodies, wreathed in red veils that pollute my flow.

Ali

I am the other brother. The modern, moderate one. The one who will not kill. Who would wish to stop it all from happening, but who will not stop the murderer.

I am the coward who disapproves in silence. I am the passive majority. I am the ordinary man, and ashamed of it. I am the brother of my sister, who cares and understands. I am the brother of my brother, who respects the authority of the firstborn. I am the one who condemns the rules but does not challenge them. My weakness makes me an accomplice.

I am the one they turn to in times of trouble, the one they tap for money. It was I who took my sisters, at Eid one year, to the big Ferris wheel in town. Their shrieks of laughter flew into the sky. Merely watching from the ground gave me vertigo. I hadn't dared go up with them.

I am the open-minded, tolerant brother, verging on liberal. A decent sort. That is my personal legend, which I fashioned, which I protect. One time I took my sister to Baghdad without her abaya. Not a word to Amir, it'll be our secret. We strolled through Mansour, she was only wearing a light headscarf, a touch of lipstick, she had the air of a girl from the capital and the men were looking. I felt proud to be her brother, walking alongside, and I couldn't see any disgrace or breach of honour in my sister's painted lips and the glances of the men. When we headed home to the South, she put her big black cloak back on, but we always cherished this break as a fun and reckless escapade, a snook cocked at the rules, and it filled us with the same naughty glee as when we used to stuff our mouths with burning-hot bread from the earth oven, deaf to the scolding of our exasperated mother. Sometimes we talked about it. That April day in Baghdad remained as a glimpse of what life could be like if our women were free.

I'm a decent sort but a coward, and those rules which I condemn, which I deplore, are my excuse. I could stand up to my brother, but then *that's how our world works*, there's

nothing doing and it's not for me to defy him.
Society provides me with the perfect dodge,
and a safe haven for my personal legend.

I am a decent sort, but I won't stop my brother
from killing my sister. I am self-effacing,
hobbled by rules I condemn, distressed to be
such a swine.

*Now Gilgamesh gets up to tell his dream to
his mother, Ninsun.
'Mother, last night I had a dream. I was full
of joy, I walked through the night among
heroes,
under the shining stars.
One star, a meteor of the stuff of Anu,
fell from heaven at my feet.
I tried to lift it, but it was too heavy.
I tried to push it, but it would not move.
All the people of Uruk flocked to see it,
they jostled around and kissed its feet.
To me its attraction was like the love
of a woman.
I bent over it as over a woman, I raised it
and brought it to you,
and you yourself made it my equal.'*

Ali knows. I don't know who told him, it can only be Baneen, or perhaps he guessed. He came into the green bedroom and threw me a look like a slap. His fists were clenched, his expression hard as a stone. And yet he seemed upset. He strode around the room, he punched the wall. We both know he will not kill me. He doesn't have that violence, that death that is inside Amir. And which my own mother will condone in the name of honour. In the name of Layla, Baneen, and Baneen's unborn child. The women of the family must remain unblemished. Pure. Untouched. Even if that means bloodshed. Neither our bodies nor our honour belong to us. They are family property. The property of our fathers and brothers.

After a while, Ali stopped pacing. His back to the wall in front of me, he let himself slide down. I thought of the many times Mohammed had sat in that very spot. Happiness is so deceptive, so brief. It escapes us like sand trickling through a closed fist and we are left alone, with empty hands, a heart in ruins and a gutful of death.

I raised my eyes towards my brother. He was in tears. Over our family honour, my death, this whole wreckage of our own making. We could have been happy. We could have lived in peace. We could have lived.

Ali wept. He crawled over to me on all fours, like a child. My big brother took me in his arms and sobbed. He rocked me. In a little while, in front of Amir, he won't be able to. My eyes were dry. Since Mohammed died, I have no tears left. I felt very far away, as if I was floating. As if all this was happening to someone else. As if I was already dead.

Layla

I am the woman to come. She for whom this killing is performed. She whose honour must at all costs be preserved. I am the child, the youngest daughter, who never knew her father and lives under her brother's rule. I am she who was born in wartime and has never known peace.

I am hardly conscious of the drama that is unfolding; I will be presented with a consummated fact. No one can oppose Amir. No one can counter male authority.

I am the one who will be coaxed and comforted. In due course I will be told not to say a certain name, to refrain from any mention of a sister who will never have existed.

In this family, a dishonoured woman is a stain that can only be washed away with blood. Spadefuls of sand will be flung over her body and her memory, she will be abandoned to the desert winds and December rains, until together we can believe that she never existed at all.

*Let the great ones of strong-walled Uruk,
let the people of Uruk weep for you,
they who pointed at us and blessed us.
Their lamentation echoes through the
countryside.
May the bear and the hyena weep for you,
the tiger and the panther, the jackal, the lion,
the buck and the doe,
and all the creatures of the plain.
May the river Ula along whose banks we used
to walk weep for you.
May the Euphrates mourn you where once
we drew pure water.
Let those who first brought bread for your
eating weep for you now;
may the brothers and the sisters grieve.*

Dusk has fallen. Outside, the river has become a ribbon of silver under the moon. I am dying. I have been dead ever since that bloodstained, hurried embrace. I am dead like all Iraqi women are dead, doomed from birth. This veil is already a prison, this night a tomb. My brother, a murderer.

Mother is still in Najaf. She will be back tomorrow. Will I see her again. Will Amir delay the execution until her return. Will my fate be held up as a lesson to the young women of the town, or will the matter be settled discreetly, behind our walls.

In the kitchen, Baneen is preparing the evening meal. It is quite strange to think that in a little while I will be dead, and they will sit down to supper.

I am in the green bedroom. Layla just came in, she was crying, she doesn't understand. She is beginning to understand. Later she will be forbidden to say my name. I will be erased, forgotten, I will never have existed. I think of Mohammed, whose body disappeared beneath Mosul. It still hurts, my love, to think of that body crushed under the rubble, incinerated, annihilated.

I wait for the sound of the car stopping in the alley. The slam of the door, the footsteps, my brother, my killer.

The earth still shakes inside my belly.

Dusk has fallen. All is dark. Over there, in the alleyway, in the house by the riverbank, she waits for death in the green bedroom.

And suddenly a terrible anguish overwhelms her as she no longer feels so sure she didn't want to live, or to meet this child, and the kicking in her belly no longer seems so dreadful, and perhaps there was more life than death in it.

In the narrow alley a car door slammed and heavy steps approached the house, a little uneven, a little lopsided. Outside, the river was a ribbon of silver under the moon.

EMILIENNE MALFATTO is a journalist and photographer whose work has appeared in the *Washington Post* and *New York Times,* among other places. She studied in France and Colombia, and worked for the French international news agency AFP before going freelance. She is the author of two novels, *Que sur toi se lamente le Tigre* (winner of the 2021 Prix Goncourt du Premier roman) and *Le colonel ne dort pas* (2022), as well as *Les serpents viendront pour toi,* winner of the Albert-Londres prize.

LORNA SCOTT FOX is a British journalist, critic, and translator from the French and Spanish. Her translations from the French include *Gertrude Stein, Pablo Picasso: Correspondence*, works of fiction and most lately *A Journey Across Borders and Through Identities* by Julia Kristeva. Her reportage, essays and reviews have appeared in the *London Review of Books, The Nation, El País, Times Literary Supplement*, and *Sidecar.* She lived in Mexico and Spain for 18 years and now lives in London.

Founded in 2014 Les Fugitives is a London-based independent press for contemporary literary fiction and narrative non-fiction in translation, mostly by francophone women writers critically acclaimed in France, and previously unpublished in English.

In 2021, Les Fugitives published Lauren Elkin's *No. 91/92: notes on a Parisian commute*, which spurred the creation, in 2022, of 'the quick brown fox' collection, dedicated to new writing in English.

Also published by Les Fugitives, in 'the quick brown fox' collection:

Erica van Horn
We Still Have the Telephone

In translation from the French:

Ananda Devi
Eve out of Her Ruins; The Living Days
trans. Jeffrey Zuckerman

Maylis de Kerangal
Eastbound
trans. Jessica Moore

Colette Fellous
This Tilting World
trans. Sophie Lewis

Jean Frémon
Now, Now, Louison; Nativity
trans. Cole Swensen

Mireille Gansel
Translation as Transhumance
trans. Ros Schwartz

Julia Kerninon
A Respectable Occupation
trans. Ruth Diver

Camille Laurens
Little Dancer Aged Fourteen
trans. Willard Wood

Noémi Lefebvre
Blue Self-Portrait; Poetics of Work
trans. Sophie Lewis

Nathalie Léger
Suite for Barbara Loden; Exposition; The White Dress
trans. Natasha Lehrer & C. Menon; Amanda DeMarco; N. Lehrer

Lucie Paye
Absence
trans. Natasha Lehrer

Anne Serre
The Governesses; The Fool and Other Moral Tales
trans. Mark Hutchinson

Shumona Sinha
Down with the Poor!
trans. Teresa Lavender Fagan

Clara Schulmann
Chicanes
trans. Lauren Elkin *et al.*

Sylvie Weil
Selfies
trans. Ros Schwartz

· www.lesfugitives.com ·